Stories Without Words

www.enchantedlionbooks.com

First American Edition published in 2011 by
Enchanted Lion Books LLC, 20 Jay Street, Studio M-18, Brooklyn, NY 11201
Translation copyright © 2011 by Enchanted Lion Books
Originally published in France by Éditions Autrement © 2009 as
Eau glacee by Arthur Geisert
Photogravure: Dupont Photogravure, Paris
All rights reserved under International and Pan-American Copyright Conventions
Library of Congress Control Number: 2010942321 ISBN 978-1-59270-098-1
Printed in January 2011 in China by South China Printing Co. Ltd., King Yip
(Dong Guan) Printing & Packaging Factory Co. Ltd., Daning Administrative District,
Humen Town, Dong Guan City, Guangdong Province 523930

Ice

ARTHUR GEISERT

ENCHANTED LION BOOKS

NEW YORK

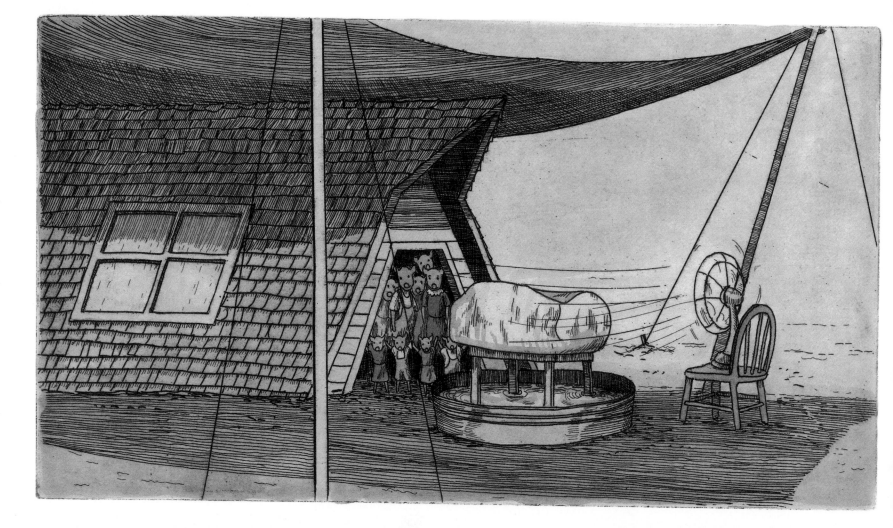